Amy the Amethyst Fairy

by Daisy Meadows

illustrated by Georgie Ripper

Join the Rainbow Magic Reading Challenge!

Read the story and collect your fairy points to climb the Reading Rainbow online. Turn to the back of the book for details!

This book is worth 5 points.

By Frosty magic I cast away
These seven jewels with their fiery rays,
So their magic powers will not be felt
And my icy castle shall not melt.

The fairies may search high and low
To find the gems and take them home.
But I will send my goblin guards
To make the fairies' mission hard.

Contents

All Set for Adventure

Welcome to Tippington Manor

"Kirsty, we're here!" Rachel Walker announced, looking out of the car window and pointing at a large sign on the wall which read *Welcome to Tippington Manor*.

Kirsty Tate, Rachel's best friend, was peering up at the cloudy sky. "I hope it's not going to rain," she said anxiously.

Then the house itself caught her eye. "Oh, look, Rachel, there's the house! Isn't it lovely?"

At the bottom of the long, sweeping gravel drive stood Tippington Manor, a huge Victorian house with an enormous wooden door, rows of tall windows and ivy rambling all over its old red bricks. The house was surrounded by gardens full of flowers and spreading trees, their autumn leaves glowing in shades of red and gold.

"Look over there, Kirsty," Rachel said to her friend as Mr Walker turned into the car park. "An adventure playground!"

Kirsty looked in the direction Rachel was pointing, and was delighted to spy the playground on a hill behind the house. She could see some tyres dangling on ropes, a silver slide and what looked like a big wooden tree-house in the centre, built around a towering oak tree.

"Isn't it great?" Kirsty whispered to Rachel, as they climbed out of the car. "The fairies would love that tree-house!"

Rachel grinned and nodded. She and Kirsty were the only people in the world who were friends with the fairies! Whenever there was trouble in Fairyland the two girls tried to help sort things out.

The fairies' biggest trouble-maker was cold, icy Jack Frost, who had recently stolen the seven magic jewels from the Queen of Fairyland's tiara. Because these gems controlled much of the magic in Fairyland, greedy Jack Frost had wanted them for himself. But when the glowing heat and light of the jewels had begun to melt his ice castle, Jack Frost had flung them out into the human world in a fit of rage.

The Jewel Fairies

To Enid and Miriam,
my fairy grandmothers

Special thanks to
Narinder Dhami

ORCHARD BOOKS

First published in Great Britain in 2005 by Orchard Books
This edition published in 2016 by The Watts Publishing Group

3 5 7 9 10 8 6 4 2

© 2016 Rainbow Magic Limited.
© 2016 HIT Entertainment Limited.
Illustrations © Georgie Ripper 2005

HiT entertainment

A CIP catalogue record for this book is available from the British Library.

ISBN 978 1 40834 876 5

Printed and bound by CPI Group (UK) Ltd, Croydon, CR0 4YY

The paper and board used in this book are made from wood from responsible sources

Orchard Books
An imprint of Hachette Children's Group
Part of The Watts Publishing Group Limited
Carmelite House, 50 Victoria Embankment, London EC4Y 0DZ

An Hachette UK Company
www.hachette.co.uk
www.hachettechildrens.co.uk

The fairies had asked Rachel and
Kirsty to help them find the jewels, and
return them to the Queen's tiara. But
Jack Frost had sent his mean goblin
servants to guard the gems, which
made getting them back a
whole lot more difficult.

"I can see where you
two want to go first!"
Mrs Walker laughed,
as Kirsty and Rachel
stared eagerly at the
tree-house. "Let's find
the orchids, then you
can go and explore the
playground while your
dad and I look at the
flowers. They have a very
famous orchid collection here."

"Orchids are Dad's favourite flowers,"
Rachel told Kirsty, rolling her eyes.
"He's mad about them!"

Mr Walker laughed. "They're very
beautiful and unusual," he explained.
"But a lot of them are tropical plants,
so they need to be kept in greenhouses."

A wooden signpost pointed in the
direction of the orchid houses, so the
girls followed Mr and Mrs Walker down
the twisting path which skirted the
beautiful gardens.

The path took them along a shady
avenue, lined with trees and marble
statues, to the bottom of a hill. There
they found three large glass greenhouses
filled with orchids, and a little shop
selling plants.

"You girls have fun," Mr Walker said
with a smile. "We'll meet you back here
in an hour."

Rachel and Kirsty waved, and headed
towards the playground.

"I wonder when we'll find the next
magic jewel," Kirsty said thoughtfully.
"We only have a few more days before
I have to go home."

"Don't worry, we'll find them all,"
Rachel said in a determined voice.
"I know we will."

At that moment, the sun broke
through the grey clouds and began
to shine brightly. The cold, crisp air
immediately seemed a little warmer.
"That's better!" Rachel said, smiling
in the sunshine.

The girls reached the playground.
"There's no-one else here," Kirsty said
happily, looking around.

"That's great!" laughed Rachel. "It's
like our very own, private adventure
playground!"

Apart from the swings, there was a big slide, a sandpit, and a maze made of tyres and rope ladders. But right in the middle of the playground was the biggest and best tree-house the girls had ever seen.

It was built around the trunk of a huge, old oak, and it was painted green with little round windows cut out of the walls here and there.

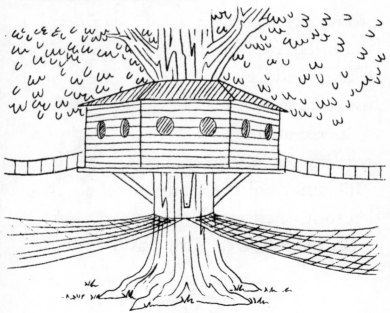

There were four other trees surrounding the oak, each with wooden bridges attached to them. These bridges made a circle around the central trunk, while two more bridges led from outer trees directly to the tree-house itself. Safety nets were strung between the bridges to make sure nobody would get hurt if they fell.

"Look at the tree-house!" Kirsty gasped. "It's amazing! Let's climb up to it, shall we?"

Rachel followed Kirsty over to the

tree-house. "Look, there's only one way
to get to it," she said, pointing to a
ladder attached to one of the
trees in the outer ring.
"You go first, Kirsty."
Kirsty began to climb
the ladder, with
Rachel close behind.
When they reached
the top, they were
near one of the
two bridges which
led right to the
tree-house itself.
"This is great," Kirsty
said happily, as they
walked across the bridge,
holding onto the rope rail.
"And we've got it all to ourselves!"

As they reached the tree-house, Rachel suddenly felt a sharp tug at the back of her head, as if somebody had pulled her hair. She stopped and turned round to see that the pink ribbon from her ponytail was dangling from a branch overhanging the bridge.

"Hang on, Kirsty!" she called to her friend, who was already inside the tree-house. "The ribbon from my ponytail's just come out. It got caught on a twig as we were crossing the bridge."

Kirsty turned to look. "Quick, go and grab it before the breeze blows it away," she urged.

Rachel was just about to step back onto the bridge, when something very strange happened. The bridge began to shimmer and flicker, and for a moment parts of it seemed to disappear!

Rachel and Kirsty blinked in surprise, and when they looked again the bridge had reappeared, looking just as solid and normal as ever.

"Did you see that, Kirsty?" Rachel gasped.

"Yes, I did!" replied Kirsty, hardly able to believe her eyes. "Do you think—?"

But before she could say anything else, the bridge began to flicker out of sight again. The girls rubbed their eyes in disbelief, but this time it didn't come back. The bridge had completely vanished!

Now You See It, Now You Don't!

"It's gone!" Rachel said in amazement. She peered out across the safety net, but there was no sign of the bridge they had just crossed. "Do you think it could be fairy magic?"

Kirsty smiled. "Maybe one of the magic jewels is nearby," she suggested. "Doesn't one of them control appearing and disappearing magic?"

"Yes," Rachel agreed excitedly. "Amy's Amethyst! Maybe it's in the tree-house."

"If it is, we'll have to be on the look-out for goblins," Kirsty reminded her.

Rachel nodded. "I don't know how I'm going to get my ribbon back," she sighed, staring at the ribbon which was still dangling from the branch. "I can't reach it without the bridge." Suddenly her eyes widened in horror. "Kirsty, however are we going to get down again? That bridge led to the ladder!"

"Don't worry," Kirsty replied. She turned and pointed to the second bridge from the tree-house door, which stretched away in the opposite direction. "After we've searched the tree-house, we'll go that way.  Then we can walk round the outer circle of bridges, and get back to the ladder again."

"Oh, yes," Rachel agreed, looking relieved. "Of course we can."

"Rachel! Kirsty!" sang out a silvery voice.

The girls spun round at the sound of the sweet, clear voice, to see a tiny

fairy swinging from Rachel's ribbon
and waving at them. She wore dark
purple trousers, with a lilac smock top
and dainty lilac shoes. Her wand was a
glittering mauve and she wore her light
brown curly hair tied up in a ponytail,
decorated with three purple flowers.

"It's Amy the Amethyst Fairy!" Kirsty gasped.

Amy freed Rachel's ribbon from the branch. Then, smiling all over her face, she floated gracefully down towards the girls, the pink ribbon streaming out behind her like a banner.

"I'm so glad you're here, girls," she said, landing lightly on Kirsty's shoulder. "I need your help."

"Thank you, Amy," Rachel said gratefully, taking the ribbon which Amy was holding out to her. "Do you think your Amethyst is nearby?"

Amy nodded. "I'm sure it is," she
replied. "I can sense that it's not far
away, now I just need to find its
hiding place."

"We saw that bridge disappear,"
explained Kirsty, pointing at the spot
where the bridge had been. "One
minute it was there, and then it
was gone!"

Amy looked very excited. "I knew I
could feel my
Amethyst working
its magic!" she
cried, dancing
up and down
on Kirsty's
shoulder. "Have
you seen any
goblins around?"

"Not yet," Kirsty replied. "We were just going to search the tree-house for your Amethyst."

"Let's look right away!" said Amy, fluttering towards the door.

Kirsty and Rachel followed her in. The tree-house was quite big but there wasn't much inside, just some benches, a little wooden table and the thick trunk of the oak tree growing through the middle of the room. It didn't take Amy and the girls very long to realise that the Amethyst wasn't there.

"Oh, dear," Amy sighed, her wings drooping. "I was so sure we'd find it here."

"Don't worry, Amy," Kirsty comforted her. "We can search all the bridges, and the trees too. Talking of bridges, I wonder if the one that vanished has come back yet?"

While Kirsty glanced out of the window to see that the bridge had still not reappeared, Rachel stared out of the opposite window to make sure that nothing else had vanished. But suddenly a flash of light caught her eye. Was she imagining it, or had she just seen a dazzling purple sparkle in the branches of one of the trees?

Rachel blinked and stared hard. There it was again! "Kirsty! Amy!" she cried, "I can see something shining in that tree – and it's purple!"

Kirsty and Amy rushed over to the window. Like Rachel, they could both see a purple something, glittering and glimmering in the sunshine.

"It must be my Amethyst!" Amy gasped, twirling round madly in the air with excitement.

"Let's go and look," said Kirsty, heading to the door.

The two girls hurried outside with Amy flying alongside them. The tree where Rachel had spotted the Amethyst was at the end of the other bridge which connected the tree-house to the outer circle.

"I hope this bridge doesn't disappear," Kirsty said anxiously, as they hurried across it.

"Girls, I can see my Amethyst!" Amy cried joyfully. "It's up there, on that crooked branch."

The girls looked where Amy was pointing. Sure enough, they could see a large, deep, purple jewel sitting on the branch. In the sunshine it glowed and winked with a rich, lilac light.

"Oh, it's beautiful!" Kirsty breathed.

Suddenly, Rachel stopped in her tracks.

"What's that noise?" she asked,
looking round.

"Ha ha ha! Hee hee hee!" somebody
sniggered.

Rachel grabbed Kirsty's arm. "Look!"
she cried, pointing ahead of them.

A grinning goblin, wearing thick gloves, was perched on the branch above the jewel. As the girls and Amy watched in horror, he leaned down and reached out to grab the Amethyst.

Amethyst Alert!

Before the girls or Amy could do anything, the goblin snatched the Amethyst and held it high above his head.

"The Amethyst is mine!" he cackled, dancing gleefully up and down on the branch. "Hurrah!"

"We must get it back!" Amy gasped,

swooping forwards. "Quickly, girls!"

Rachel and Kirsty dashed after her. But before they reached the tree, the goblin raced off around the outer circle of bridges. When he reached the next tree, he stopped and glanced back over his shoulder.

"Can't catch me!" he sneered, pulling a face at them. Then he took off again, running right round the central tree-house.

"Kirsty," Rachel panted, as they gave chase, "he's heading towards the ladder to the ground. He's going to escape!"

"Oh, no!" Kirsty groaned, seeing that Rachel was right.

The goblin was looking very pleased with himself as he pelted headfirst towards the last bridge and the ladder which led down to the ground. But all of a sudden, the last bridge began to blur and flicker. Just before the goblin reached it, it vanished into thin air!

"Ohhh!" The goblin cried, taken by surprise. He tried to stop, but he was going so fast that he skidded right into the tree to which the bridge had been attached. "Ouch!" he grumbled, rubbing his nose. "That hurt!"

"We've got him!" Rachel yelled triumphantly. "That tree doesn't have a bridge to the tree-house. His only way out now is to come back past us."

"Give me back my Amethyst!" cried Amy, fluttering towards the goblin with a determined look on her face.

The goblin glanced at her sulkily. "Shan't!" he told Amy. But he looked around in confusion, gazing at the empty space where the bridge had been, and then at Amy and the girls who were hurrying towards him.

"Over here!" yelled a new voice. Someone was shouting from the central tree-house in a rough, gruff voice.

Amy, Rachel and Kirsty turned round, and were dismayed to see two green, warty-faced goblins. They were leaning out of the tree-house windows, waving at the goblin who held the Amethyst. One of them was wearing gloves.

"Over here!" the one with the gloves was shrieking. "Throw it to meeeee!"

Amy, Rachel and Kirsty watched in horror as the goblin nearest to them drew back his arm and hurled the Amethyst through the air. The glowing jewel went spinning and tumbling towards the tree-house. As it passed, branches, ropes and leaves mysteriously appeared and disappeared, and a glittering trail of purple sparkles crackled in its wake.

"Quick!" Rachel shouted. "Back to

the tree-house!"

The girls began racing round the circle of bridges again, as the goblin in the tree-house leaned out and caught the jewel.

He gave a screech of triumph. "I've got the Amethyst now!" he yelled gleefully to the friends. "And you're not getting it back!"

"We have to stop those goblins!" panted Kirsty.

"There's only one way they can go," Rachel replied, stopping as they reached the end of the bridge which led from the outer circle back to the tree-house. "And it's this way!"

At that moment, the two goblins dashed out of the house, and Kirsty realised that Rachel was right. Because the other bridge had disappeared, there was only one bridge left leading from the tree-house – and she, Rachel and Amy were standing right at the end of it!

The goblins stopped, looking very cross when they saw Amy and the girls blocking their path. They began whispering to each other. The next moment, they swung themselves over the edge of the bridge and dropped down onto the safety net underneath. Then they began clambering across the net towards the exit ladder.

"Oh, no!" Amy cried. "Those nasty goblins are escaping with my Amethyst!"

Kirsty Swings into Action

Kirsty turned to the little fairy. "Amy, can you make Rachel and me fairy-sized?" she asked. "Then we won't have to worry about the bridges appearing and disappearing."

Amy nodded and waved her wand in the air. A shower of lilac-coloured sparkles fell softly onto Rachel and

Kirsty, turning them into tiny fairies with shimmering wings.

"We're all too small to steal the Amethyst back now," Amy pointed out. "What are we going to do?"

"We can distract the goblins and stop them from escaping," Kirsty replied. "That will give us time to think of a way to get the jewel."

"Maybe we can make them drop it," suggested Rachel.

"Good idea," Amy agreed.

Kirsty, Rachel and Amy flew down
and hovered around the goblins' heads.
The first goblin had managed to join
his two friends now, but all three of
them were in a very bad mood because
their big feet kept getting
stuck in the safety net.

"Pesky fairies!"
the one holding
the Amethyst
shouted. He hit
out wildly at
Rachel, but
missed her by
a long way. "Go away!"

"Help, I'm stuck!" shouted another.

Amy had flown at him, and he'd
fallen over backwards. "My feet are
caught in the holes," he wailed.

The other two ignored him. They were too busy trying to scramble on across the net towards the exit ladder.

Amy and the girls fluttered around the head of the goblin with the Amethyst, doing their best to make him drop the jewel. Unfortunately, he was clinging to it determinedly and the friends didn't seem to be making much progress.

Suddenly, Kirsty noticed a long, thick rope hanging down in front of her. She was sure it hadn't been there before, and realised that it must have appeared thanks to the Amethyst's magic. The dangling rope gave Kirsty an idea, and she waved at Rachel and Amy.

"Quick! Back to the tree-house!" she cried breathlessly, grabbing the end of the rope and zooming up into the air with it.

"But the goblins are getting away!" Rachel argued.

"I know, so hurry!" Kirsty insisted. "I've got an idea."

Amy and Rachel followed Kirsty back to the tree-house.

As soon as they landed, Kirsty turned to Amy. "Can you make us human-sized again?" she panted.

Amy nodded and raised her wand once more. As soon as the girls were back to

their normal sizes, Kirsty got a firm grip
on the rope. Then, taking
a deep breath, she
leaned backwards
and swung herself
off the tree-house
platform and
out over the
safety net.

"Kirsty, be
careful!" Rachel
and Amy both
called anxiously.

As Kirsty flew
through the air, she
saw that the goblins
had almost reached the
tree with the exit ladder.
They were looking extremely pleased

with themselves, and hadn't noticed
her clinging to the rope and
swinging in their direction.
As they laughed and
slapped each other
on the back,
Kirsty swung
silently towards
the goblin
who held the
Amethyst, her
hand outstretched.
She knew she
had to be quick,
because she'd only
get one chance…
As Kirsty swept past the
goblin, she deftly snatched the magic
Amethyst right out of his gloved hand!

The goblin's eyes almost popped out of his head, and he gave a scream of rage. "Give that back!" he roared.

"I don't think so!" Kirsty yelled, clutching the jewel tightly as the rope carried her back towards the tree-house where her friends were waiting.

As soon as she could reach, Rachel grabbed Kirsty and pulled her safely back onto the platform.

"My Amethyst!" Amy declared joyfully, fluttering down to stare at the jewel which was glowing in Kirsty's hand.

"And look," Rachel cried, her eyes wide with amazement. "The bridge is back!"

Kirsty and Amy turned to look. The first bridge to the exit ladder, which the girls had crossed to reach the tree-house, had now reappeared.

"That means we can get out of here right away," Kirsty said happily, heading off across the bridge. "Come on!"

Rachel and Amy followed her. But as they stepped onto the bridge, three very angry and grim-faced goblins appeared at the other end. They were completely blocking the friends' escape.

Trapped!

"We're trapped!" Kirsty gasped, looking around for a way out.

But it was no use. Two of the goblins were dashing along the bridge towards them, while the other stood guard at the exit ladder.

"You can't get away!" one goblin yelled. "So give us the Amethyst!"

"Never!" Amy cried bravely.

Rachel looked around desperately for something to help them escape from the goblins. Suddenly, her eye fell on the silver slide on the other side of the playground. She turned to Amy. "Amy, could you use your magic to make a slide appear?" she asked. "Then we could slide safely down to the ground."

Amy nodded and lifted her wand. A
swirl of lilac sparkles cascaded to
the ground, and there was a
flash of purple smoke. Then,
between the safety nets,
appeared a beautiful,
shiny, helter-skelter
slide, spiralling all the
way to the ground.

"Great idea, Rachel!"
Kirsty gasped, clutching
the Amethyst tightly
and leaping
onto the slide.

"Hurry!" Amy
urged the girls, as
she hovered anxiously
over their heads. "The
goblins are right behind us!"

Kirsty pushed herself off, as Rachel climbed on behind her. The slide was super-smooth, and Kirsty found herself whizzing along at great speed, her hair streaming out behind. She landed safely at the bottom, and jumped off, just in time to stop Rachel sliding into the back of her.

"Quickly, girls!" Amy flew down and landed on Kirsty's shoulder. "The goblins are coming!"

Rachel and Kirsty began to run away underneath the safety nets. But to their dismay the goblins were already whizzing down the slide after them.

"Ouch! Ow!" they yelled crossly, as they bumped into each other at the bottom. They rolled off onto the grass, picked themselves up and raced after the girls.

"They're getting closer!" Kirsty panted as she ducked underneath another safety net. "How are we going to get away?"

Amy smiled. "This time I have an idea!" she whispered, with a cheeky smile.

Rachel and Kirsty watched curiously as Amy first touched the tip of her wand to the magic Amethyst, and then flew up to lightly touch her wand to the safety net. The disappearing and appearing magic of the Amethyst began to work, and the knots in the ties holding up the net began to vanish. Amid a dazzling shower of lilac sparks, the net slowly came free of its ties.

As the goblins dashed towards Rachel and Kirsty, the net began to float downwards. Realising what Amy had in mind, the girls darted out from underneath the net just in time. Down it came, right on top of the goblins!

Goblin Tangle

The goblins roared with fury and struggled to free themselves, but as they thrashed about they only got more and more tangled up in the net. Soon they were arguing with each other.

"Help!" cried one.

"My nose is stuck!" yelled another.

"Get your foot out of my ear!" shouted the third.

Rachel and Kirsty stood watching them, and couldn't help laughing. "Well done, Amy," said Kirsty. "It's going to take ages for them to untangle themselves!"

"And by then my Amethyst will be back in Queen Titania's tiara," Amy said happily. She touched the tip of her wand to the jewel in Kirsty's hand, releasing a spark of purple fire. Then she waved her wand expertly in the air, and another safety net magically appeared to replace the one which held the goblins.

"Now nobody playing in the
tree-house will fall and get hurt," Amy
announced, firmly. Kirsty and Rachel
watched as she waved
her wand over the
Amethyst one last
time and sent it
swiftly back to
Fairyland in a swirl
of fiery purple sparks.

"Thank you so much, girls," Amy
went on. She fluttered onto Kirsty's
shoulder, and then onto Rachel's,
planting soft kisses on their cheeks.
"Now the Amethyst is back where it
belongs, and I must go home."

"We'd better go, too, Kirsty," said
Rachel, glancing at her watch. "It's
time to meet Mum and Dad."

Kirsty smiled at their fairy friend. "Goodbye, Amy."

Amy waved her wand at the girls and zoomed up into the sky. "Goodbye, girls!" she called in her silvery voice. "Don't forget, we're counting on you to find the other magic jewels!"

Kirsty and Rachel nodded and waved and then hurried out of the adventure playground.

"That was fun!" Rachel said with a grin, as they ran down the hill. "But I was really afraid the goblins were going to get away with the jewel this time."

"So was I," Kirsty agreed. "Look, there's your mum and dad."

Mr and Mrs Walker were just strolling out of the garden shop. The girls raced over to join them.

"What have you got there, Dad?" Rachel asked curiously, noticing that her dad was carrying something very carefully.

"It's an orchid." Mr Walker replied, pulling back the tissue paper which was wrapped around the plant pot. "I bought it in the shop. Isn't it beautiful?"

Rachel and Kirsty stared at the exotic-looking purple flower.

"It's exactly the same colour as Amy's Amethyst!" Kirsty whispered to Rachel with a smile.

"It's lovely, Dad," Rachel told him, smiling too.

Mr and Mrs Walker took the orchid over to the car, and Rachel and Kirsty followed.

"So, now we've found our fifth jewel," Kirsty said happily, "Queen Titania's tiara is almost complete again!"

"Yes, only two more gems left to find," Rachel agreed thoughtfully. "I wonder where they can be."

Now it's time for Kirsty and Rachel to help...

Sophie the Sapphire Fairy

Read on for a sneak peek...

"I wish this rain would stop," Kirsty Tate said to her friend, Rachel Walker, as they splashed through the puddles on the busy shopping street. "My trainers are soaked."
She pulled the rainbow-coloured umbrella she was holding further down over their heads.

"Mine, too," Rachel said. "Still, I'm glad we came into town today. I got the perfect present for Danny's birthday party next week." She swung the shopping bag she was holding. It contained a bright red, turbo-charged water pistol that Rachel was sure Danny, her six-year-old cousin, would love.

"I wish I was going to be here for his party," sighed Kirsty.

"Me too. I can't believe you're going home tomorrow," Rachel told her. "This week's gone so quickly."

"Too quickly," replied Kirsty. "I just hope we find another jewel today."

The two girls exchanged a look. They shared an incredible secret. They were best friends with the fairies! They'd helped the fairies out lots of times in the past when nasty Jack Frost had been causing trouble. Now they'd been asked to help again.

This time, Jack Frost had stolen seven

magic jewels from Queen Titania's tiara. The jewels controlled special fairy powers and the fairies needed them back so that they could recharge their magic wands. But Jack Frost had banished the jewels to the human world and sent his mean goblin servants to guard them.

Rachel and Kirsty had already helped five of the Jewel Fairies get their magic jewels back, but there were still two gems missing – the Sapphire that controlled wishing magic, and the Diamond that controlled flying magic...

Read Sophie the Sapphire Fairy to find out what adventures are in store for Kirsty and Rachel!

Meet the
Jewel Fairies

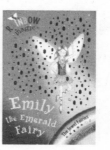

Join Rachel and Kirsty as they hunt for the
jewels that naughty Jack Frost has stolen
from Queen Titania's crown!

www.rainbowmagicbooks.co.uk

RAINBOW magic

Calling all parents, carers and teachers!
The Rainbow Magic fairies are here to help
your child enter the magical world of reading.
Whatever reading stage they are at, there's
a Rainbow Magic book for everyone!
Here is Lydia the Reading Fairy's guide to
supporting your child's journey at all levels.

Starting Out

1

Our Rainbow Magic Beginner Readers are perfect for first-time readers who are just beginning to develop reading skills and confidence. Approved by teachers, they contain a full range of educational levelling, as well as lively full-colour illustrations.

Developing Readers

2

Rainbow Magic Early Readers contain longer stories and wider vocabulary for building stamina and growing confidence. These are adaptations of our most popular Rainbow Magic stories, specially developed for younger readers in conjunction with an Early Years reading consultant, with full-colour illustrations.

Going Solo

3

The Rainbow Magic chapter books – a mixture of series and one-off specials – contain accessible writing to encourage your child to venture into reading independently. These highly collectible and much-loved magical stories inspire a love of reading to last a lifetime.

www.rainbowmagicbooks.co.uk

"Rainbow Magic got my daughter reading chapter books. Great sparkly covers, cute fairies and traditional stories full of magic that she found impossible to put down" – Mother of Edie (6 years)

"Florence LOVES the Rainbow Magic books. She really enjoys reading now" Mother of Florence (6 years)

Read along the Reading Rainbow!

Well done – you have completed the book!

This book was worth 1 star.

See how far you have climbed on the Reading Rainbow.
The more books you read, the more stars you can colour in
and the closer you will be to becoming a Royal Fairy!

Do you want to print your own Reading Rainbow?

1) Go to the Rainbow Magic website

2) Download and print out the poster

3) Colour in a star for every book you finish
and climb the Reading Rainbow

4) For every step up the rainbow,
you can download your very own certificate

There's all this and lots more at
rainbowmagicbooks.co.uk

You'll find activities, stories, a special newsletter
AND you can search for the fairy with your name!